1975

MCMLXXV

Author:
Bill Webb

Editor:
Jeff Harkness?

Layout:
Suzy Moseby

Front Cover Art:
Michael Syrigos

Cover Design
Jim Wampler

Cartography:
Robert Altbauer

Project Manager:
Zach Glazar

Pathfinder Conversion:
Michael Mars Russell

Frog God Games is:

Bill Webb, Matt Finch, Zach Glazar, Charles A. Wright, Edwin Nagy, Mike Badolato, and John Barnhouse

FROG GOD GAMES
ISBN: 1-62283-893-6
PF PoD

Table of Contents

1975
MCMLXXV

By Bill Webb

A Pathfinder 1e adventure designed for four to six characters of 1st to 3rd level

MCMLXXV

Converting 1975 for Pathfinder

As you read through the first few pages of this module, you'll notice there are references to **Swords and Wizardry**. This is intentional. I wanted to make sure that the inspiration for this module was untouched through conversion and that the primer on old school play was left intact. The content that follows that section is converted for Pathfinder. Any creatures, hazards, or new magic items encountered are either in the PF SRD or in the Appendix in this module.

When Bill wrote this module, he wanted to share with everyone something that was special to him, and that was a part of his experience with RPGs. I too want to share that with you all. While my experience in old school roleplaying is nowhere near as extensive as Bill's — I started playing in 2005 and have been GMing ever since. My experience with old school came later than most, but I fell in love with the style of it. My home game has been running 7 years with the same group, more or less, and the deaths are less often now, but sometimes a clever trap or hidden item will surprise them and that is where the fun lives.

Given the spirit of this module, you'll notice that many of the encounters are not winnable by a group of 4-6 characters of 1st to 3rd level. There are also traps that will outright kill a low-level character (depending on death rules you utilize in your game, that is). That is the way it was with old school games. There was wisdom in running away and figuring out how to avoid combat, or to use the environment against a challenging encounter, and in also realizing that the players should have a good time but also be challenged. The players in my weekly Pathfinder home game have learned these lessons, often the hard way. I hope this conversion presents an opportunity for you and your players to experience some of the nostalgia of old school gaming.

Michael Russell
February 2019

Old School Gaming

This module is intended to show how old school roleplaying provides enhanced descriptions and provides not only storyline and encounters but creates a feeling of "being there." I have borrowed from work I did supporting Matt Finch at North Texas RPG Con in 2011, as well as sessions I ran at PaizoCon in 2011 and 2012. Kudos to Tabletop Adventures (http://www.tabletopadventures.com/) for the great work they have put in over the years in providing table ready description text. Back in the old days, this was the way it was done—on the fly, by the old timers (and this author counts himself an "old timer").

Rules were few, people did not really understand roleplaying games as they do today, and we had to make them smell, hear and feel the stench of the dead body, the weird drumming sounds in the deep, and the cold, clammy touch of a ghoul's claw.

When the game was new, none of the players had read 100+ RPG books. They did not know if a dwarf was a 6-inch tall faerie or one of Tolkien's hardened miners with an axe and a love of gold. We had to tell them. As the game has evolved, we deal with a much more educated and cunning set of players. In order to stay a step ahead, the game master must create and describe many situations both hazardous and benign with equal enthusiasm. Players can be kept on their toes and edges of their seats by harmless blue flowers as well as deadly poisonous yellow flowers if they don't know which flower is which. The art of storytelling in our favorite game is not dead—heavens no—but to really get back to the roots of the game, it helps to provide mystery and fear.

Some players have joked with me over the years that they never know when to let up—and instead assume combat mode as soon as "flavor text" gets heavy. Having personally never been a fan of the "spot check" or a blind roll to "disarm the trap" without having it fully described, I use flavor text to allow players to creatively solve problems by asking questions and better understanding "what it is" that their characters see and do. Secret doors are not automatically opened…they must be examined, loose bricks and levers must be searched for, and so on. An orc is not just an orc. It could be a hairy humanoid, with jutting tusks and whitish green skin, barking in an obscene, unintelligible language while it charges at you with its rusted poleaxe! The troll does not simply "regenerate", but its wounds close over the arrows in its chest almost faster than the blood drips from them.

This is the stuff of 1975.

I have tried in this module to provide a judge with enough information to improvise and make the most of description as a technique in his or her game. Resources exist (Tabletop Adventures, and our very own *Tome of Adventure Design* come to mind) to add to this as deemed needed. It's not the only way, nor the best way to play. It's just how I play, and I play **Swords and Wizardry**.

This adventure is designed for 4-6 characters of levels 1-4. The setting may seem fairly easy for characters above 1st level, however, I would enjoin upon the judge to play his or her monsters to kill. Treat them as if they were your own player characters. A goblin with a bow would never get near Joe Platemail III with his huge sword and slow movement rate. A crocodile would grab a lightly armed opponent and drag them into the water—it would never stand and fight a group of 5 men toe to toe. Ghouls would paralyze one opponent and then move to the next, zombies would well, ok, they would act like zombies and just stand there and attack.

Two things make fairly played monsters in my games. One is that I play them as smart as they are, and the second is that I roll all dice openly on the table for all to see, and mandate that all do the same. Oddly, people think I am discouraging player cheating. In reality, I find (even in my own case at times) it's the DM who more frequently dances the dice to keep characters alive. Give these things a shot and see what the results are. I have found that the players are more in love with the challenge of the game and less in love with their characters. Likewise, a player who has reached higher levels (as high as 4!) has truly made an achievement.

On the player's side, it is of critical importance, at least to me, that they learn how to run as well as fight. As Gandalf said, "there is always something bigger in this world than yourself". Truly skilled old school players employed many means of evasion as well as tricky means of fighting the bad guys. Old rules even included methods for increasing odds (gold pieces thrown behind for intelligent monsters, food for the less intelligent monsters), and just because it was "there" did not mean you had to kill it—at least yet. Players would base entire game sessions and plans on taking out a single BEBG (big evil bad guy) that they had previously escaped from.

That is why speed, evasion and care are required. As experience points (XP) for slaying monsters are few, and for gathering loot are big, it made far more sense to avoid wasted resources by killing everything that crossed one's path, and instead staying goal focused and keeping one's eye on the ball. The big monsters (intelligent ones) have big treasure (and big XP). The bugs (and purple worms) have none.

The Adventure

Now that you, as the reader, are sick of hearing this old grognard's lectures of how he runs the game, it's time to get on with the adventure. I have tried to illustrate several of the concepts I discussed above into examples of play and a scenario that will challenge and reward players for using their noggins.

The adventure begins with the characters finding a treasure map that leads them through a forested section of a river valley and down into the swamplands below. The map itself (players Map 1 and GM Map 1) show the general path to the "treasure" (in reality a small dungeon). The path taken to the dungeon may vary depending on the player's choices of travel—the GM map is coded with locations of the various encounters and other areas of interest that they could find. No path is the "right" path, although some may be easier than others.

The player's map is found in the back of the book and can be copied and given to them as a handout. The Judges map varies slightly in that it contains the map key detailing various encounter areas, and the players map just shows a dotted line. How the characters get the map is up to you as a Judge. Perhaps it was sold to the characters by a grizzled old man or found as part of another treasure hoard. In any case, the introduction to "how" they start the adventure is not detailed here.

The adventure begins as the characters leave the **[tavern, town, etc.]** and start down the road towards a valley. The valley itself is horseshoe-shaped, and the road the characters are on is near the top. The treasure map indicates that the "treasure" is in the bottom of the valley along a swampy river course and is located on an island within the swamp itself. The trick is to find a safe way through the valley to reach the swamp, then to locate the island and the treasure (really a small dungeon). The encounter areas are located on the map and can be used if the players travel near them.

Random Encounters

Random encounter checks should be made twice per day and twice per night. One way to handle this is to roll 1d12 per day and per night to randomize the hour (1 = 6 am, 12 = 5 pm at day, and 1 = 6 pm and 12 = 5 am at night) to determine when the check is made. In most terrains, a random encounter typically occurs 5% of the time (rolling a 1 on a d20). Forests increase the chance to 10% (1-2 on a d20), while there is a 20% chance (1-4 on a d20) of a random encounter occurring in the swamp or near the river.

Encounter tables are organized by terrain with descriptions of each encounter following the encounter table.

Plains Above the Valley

For random encounters in the plains above the valley, roll on the table below and refer to the appropriate description after the table.

d12	Encounter
1	Circling Birds
2	Weird Snowfall
3	Falling Star
4-5	2d4 **Bandits**
6	2d6 **Wolves**
7	Trade Caravan
8-9	Herd of Animals
10	Swarm of Insects
11	Lunatic
12	**Ankheg**

1. Circling Birds. Large carrion birds circle high above in the distance. Something must have died.

You see a group of birds circling a mile distant. One by one, the birds drop to the ground. If approached, and before they can see what the birds are doing, they smell the cloying odor of rotting flesh. The birds sit pecking at the corpse of a large elk.

If the characters approach the carcass, the following can be read:

The birds squawk and shift around the body but do not give up their feast. One, sitting on the head of the dead creature, eyes them balefully.

2. Weird Snowfall. There are thousands of tiny seeds covering the ground, each surrounded by a gossamer sphere of tiny white fluff that helps it float lightly in the air. But the moment they move, it shifts and rises in ways snow never does. As they brush it off, it hovers in the air, gradually settling. They came, apparently, from the great tree (cottonwood) and covered the ground, plants, and people. They get into everything, though they do no damage. They are annoying to breathe but are only very dense right around the tree. Within a short time, although one or two can be seen still floating on the breeze, most have dispersed with the wind.

You wake in the morning to find that all the ground is white. Lying over everything is a layer of white stuff that looks like snow.

3. Falling Star (Only at night, reroll otherwise). Sometimes shooting stars do come to earth and great good fortune is said to favor those who find one. Well, fortune is certainly smiling on the players as a rock the size of a large dog sits not far from the campsite. The rock is still glowing slightly and there is a trail of blackened, scorched grass to show where it initially landed and then slid along the ground perhaps as much as fifty paces. It is too hot to handle at the moment and a rock that size is very heavy, but it is well-known that the iron from meteors can be used to make superior steel and swords made from it may have a telling advantage.

Two long swords or four shorter blades could be made from the meteor, if it can be successfully brought to a suitably skilled blacksmith. Those weapons may at your discretion have a +1 bonus to hit and damage in combat or else just be light, flexible and well-formed.

The meteor is found only once, although shooting stars can be a recurring encounter.

The night sky is bright and clear here in the grasslands. The stars themselves twinkle like diamonds in the void. Shooting stars race through the night, first white and then darkening to orange. It looks as if they will fall to earth here and perhaps bring luck and fortune with them, but they always just disappear before they come to earth.

4-5. Bandits! The group encounters 2d4 **bandits**—it is possible the bandits were trying to ambush the party, or, depending on the time of day, the bandits could be in their camp and could be surprised by the party. Determining surprise is typically done by comparing the Stealth check of anyone attempting to hide with the Perception check of those on the opposing side.

Bandit (2d4) CR ½
XP 200
HP 11 (Pathfinder Roleplaying Game GameMastery Guide, "Bandit")

6. Wolves. The party encounters a pack of 2d6 **wolves**. Wolves seldom attack a party (unless wounded are present, or the characters number less than 1/3 the wolves number) during the day. At night, the wolves use Stealth checks to determine surprise, and attempt to gang attack 1-2 characters in hopes of a quick kill and drag off attempt. If the party has horses, the wolves attempt to kill one and then run off a short distance, having learned that dead animals are often left behind by human groups.

The howling of wolves seems to be getting closer and closer.

Wolf (2d6) CR 1
XP 400
HP 13 (Pathfinder Roleplaying Game Bestiary, "Wolf")

7. Trade Caravan. These encounters typically involve 2d6 wagons and are accompanied by 1d8 **guards**, 2 merchants (use the **noble** stat block), and 2 drivers (**commoners**) per wagon. Guards are armed with crossbows and hand weapons and typically wear chainmail. Goods range in value from 10-100 gp per wagon and usually include items of value to local villages (cloth, metal goods and sundries, farm equipment, food and drink). There is a 10% chance that the caravan is carrying adventuring supplies (such as arms or armor). If so, the number of guards is doubled.

Caravan merchants are happy to sell to or buy from the party. If a successful DC 12 Diplomacy check is made, the merchants will sell items at normal prices and buy items at 50% of their value. If the check fails, item prices are inflated to 150% of their normal value, and buying prices decrease to 25% of their normal value. Each merchant carries from 20-200 gp in cash.

The trade caravan has setup camp in a clearing near a bend in the road. Armed guards patrol the perimeter of the camp, eyes searching for signs of mischief, while the merchants busily barter with customers looking for a deal.

8-9. Herd of Animals. A herd of **deer** or otherwise innocuous beasts (**boar**, etc.) is spooked by the characters and runs by. Fast thinking players can shoot arrows and get a few free meals.

A crashing sound from the left greets you as a herd of animals burst from the thicket, spooked by your passage.

10. **Insect Swarm.** One of the characters accidentally steps on a nest of hornets or otherwise nasty, biting insects.

Wasp Swarm CR 3
XP 800
HP 31 (Pathfinder Roleplaying Game Bestiary, "Wasp Swarm")

11. **Lunatic.** A disoriented, possibly unstable elderly humanoid is lost/wandering about in the wilderness. Perhaps they are carrying a fishing pole and casting into the grass, or they are digging a large hole with a shovel, trying to unearth a "treasure" or "dungeon" and asks for help. Lawful groups would likely attempt to return the innocent to their home (usually less than 4 hours away).

12. **Ankheg.** The **ankheg** attempts to surprise the party by attacking from below and burrowing up underneath them. Compare the Perception check of each of the party members to the Stealth check of the ankheg to determine surprise. If none of the party is surprised, a successful DC 15 Perception check will reveal mounds of disturbed dirt on the ground in the area indicating that something is active nearby.

A large, praying mantis-like creature bursts from the ground.

Ankheg CR 3
XP 800
HP 28 (Pathfinder Roleplaying Game Bestiary, "Ankheg")

The huge insect has no treasure; however, its hide could be used to make one suit of high quality leather armor by a skilled armor worker. What benefits high quality armor has are up to your discretion. Possible ideas are resistance to a specific type of damage (piercing), or a bonus to AC (+1).

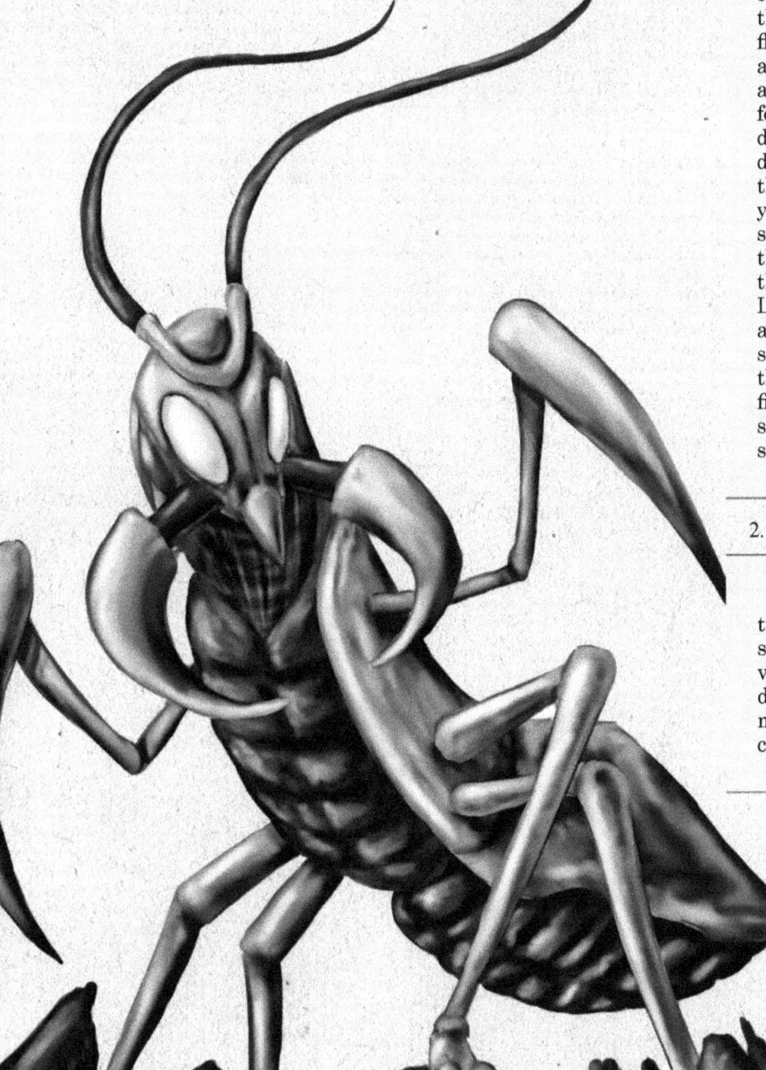

FOREST IN THE VALLEY

For random encounters in the forest in the valley, roll on the table below and refer to the appropriate description after the table.

d12	Encounter
1	Storm
2	Loud Birds
3-4	2d4 **Kobolds**
5-6	1d4 **Giant Spiders**
7	1d4 **Worgs**
8-9	Herd of Animals
10	Trap
11	Lunatic
12	**Owlbear**

1. **Storm.** Lightning, thunder, wind, rain, and a tornado! The characters should be moderately safe as long as they stay under cover.

A bolt of lightning lances down from the sky, squarely striking a small tree nearby. A shower of small wood chips fly about as the tree virtually explodes under the electrical onslaught. A few gray clouds have gathered overhead, but nothing to indicate a storm. A gigantic flash of lightning is followed immediately by a deafening clap of thunder and with a rush, the rain starts. The water pelts down mercilessly, instantly soaking everything. The rain drips under armor and through clothing. Gusts of wind whip through the grass, swirling it wildly. For a few moments, the rain comes down so hard that the area is heavily obscured. Overhead, the sky has grown completely black with thick clouds, and each flash of lightning illuminates the boiling mass of thunderheads above. Lightning and thunder are now virtually simultaneous, and each boom shakes the ground. The torrent continues for what feels like hours, and then quickly dies off with a few final stinging drops. The rain passes, though the clouds overhead promise to deliver more. Flashes of lightning still burst in the sky, but the thunder sounds farther away. The sky has a sickly greenish-yellow cast to it, turning the clouds an unearthly shade. After some time, a sudden change takes place. The clouds darken, and the wind begins whipping ferociously. Sheets of rain fall from the sky drenching everything, followed closely by heavy hail. Lightning streaks across the sky; the black clouds are piled high above you. A roaring sound is heard, and the ground begins to shake. A writhing, grey finger of clouds begins to descend from the sky towards the earth. As it touches down, the dust of the fields mushrooms up around its base. Like a snake preparing to strike, the storm writhes its way on a parallel course to your own, spreading destruction in its wake.

---

2. **Loud Birds.** The trees above are filled with cacophonous birds.

The woods are filled with birdsong today. From the lilting twitters of tiny, brightly feathered finches to the throaty calls of surly crows, the birds all seem to be trying to outdo each other in volume and persistence. Above there are glimpses of the singers darting away from the group to continue their serenades from more secluded branches. The music is at times lovely, other times cacophonous. The one thing it never is, is silent.

3-4. **Kobolds.** The party encounters a group of 2d4 kobolds. These nasty little buggers are full of tricks and surprises. Whether the kobolds surprise the party or not, they have laid an elaborate ambush designed to give them every advantage.

Kobold (2d4) CR ¼
XP 100
HP 5 (Pathfinder Roleplaying Game Bestiary, "Kobold")

Each kobold carries a spear and sling with 20 bullets, as well as one of the following items that they will definitely use during combat:

d6	Item
1	A poisonous snake on a 5-foot pole (snake is 2 hp, attacks separately, save at +2 or die)
2	1d2 oil flasks and a torch and tinder box
3	Caltrops
4	A thin leather trip rope, 10 feet long
5	Has a trap set nearby and tries to lead a character into it (see encounter 10 below).
6	A vial of green slime

The kobolds will hit and run and will not engage the "big people" unless they clearly have an advantage. They carry no treasure.

Venomous Snake CR 1
XP 400
HP 2 (Pathfinder Roleplaying Game Bestiary, "Snake, Venomous")
Poison (Ex)
Bite—injury; *save* Fort DC 13; *effect* death

Green Slime CR 4
XP 1,200 (Pathfinder Roleplaying Game Core Rulebook, "Green Slime")

5-6. **Spiders.**
Without warning, 1d4 **giant spiders** descend from the trees above, possibly surprising the party. As usual, compare the Perception check of each character against the Stealth checks of each spider. Individual characters are surprised if their Perception check is not equal to or greater than the Stealth check of a spider.
If the party isn't surprised, the party should notice the webbing in the trees before they are attacked by the spiders.

Giant Spider (1d4) CR 1
XP 400
HP 16 (Pathfinder Roleplaying Game Bestiary, "Giant Spider")

7. **Worgs.** The party encounters 1d4 **worgs**. These evil creatures hunt the forest, slaying all they encounter. Typically, they will both attack the same opponent, trying to down each foe in turn. They retreat from fire if strongly presented and are intelligent enough to avoid heavily armored foes if offered a "softer" target.

Worg (1d4) CR 2
XP 600
HP 26 (Pathfinder Roleplaying Game Bestiary, "Worg")

8-9. **Herd of Animals.** A herd of **deer** or otherwise innocuous beasts (**boar**, etc.) is spooked by the characters and runs by. Fast thinking players can shoot arrows and get a few free meals.

A crashing sound from the left greets you as a herd of animals burst from the thicket, spooked by your passage.

---

10. **Trap.** One thing about woods that have kobolds in them, is that they often are filled with traps. These little devils have constructed several traps in this area. Roll 1d6 to determine the type:

d6	Trap	Effect
1	**Pit Trap CR 1/4** **XP 65** **Type** mechanical; **Perception** DC 15; **Disable Device** DC 20 **Trigger** location; **Reset** manual	10-ft.-deep pit (1d6 falling damage); DC 20 Reflex avoids; multiple targets (all targets in the trap's area)
2	**Swinging Logs Trap CR 2** **XP 600** **Type** mechanical; **Perception** DC 12; **Disable Device** DC 12 **Trigger** location; **Reset** manual	Atk +5 melee (3d6+5/×2) and knocked prone; Reflex DC 15 negates prone condition
3	**Spiked Snare CR 1** **XP 400** **Type** mechanical; **Perception** DC 20; **Disable Device** DC 15 **Trigger** touch; **Reset** manual	CMB +10 (vs. target's CMD; target gains grappled condition and is yanked 10 feet into the air); Atk +8 melee (2 spikes for 1d6+2 damage each) A caught PC can escape this snare on his own by making a DC 22 Strength or Escape Artist check, or automatically if he has a slashing weapon with which he can cut the snare line (although this action results in a 10 foot fall).
4	**Javelin Trap CR 2** **XP 600** **Type** mechanical; **Perception** DC 20; **Disable Device** DC 20 **Trigger** location; **Reset** none	Atk +15 ranged (javelin; 1d6+6)
5	**Spiked Pit Trap CR 2** **XP 600** **Type** mechanical; **Perception** DC 20; **Disable Device** DC 20 **Trigger** location; **Reset** manual	10-ft.-deep pit (1d6 falling damage); pit spikes (Atk +10 melee, 1d4 spikes per target for 1d4+2 damage each); DC 20 Reflex avoids; multiple targets (all targets in a 10-ft.-square area)
6	**Swinging Bees Nest Trap CR 3** **Wasp Swarm CR 3** **XP 800** **HP 31** (Pathfinder Roleplaying Game Bestiary, "Wasp Swarm") **Trigger** location; **Reset** manual	A **wasp swarm** appears in the space of the character. DC 13 Perception check to spot and avoid the tripwire. DC 13 Disable Device check to disarm.

11. **Lunatic.** A VERY unstable and dangerous madman who is initially encountered singing softly to themselves. This madman seems harmless until the characters bed down or are otherwise unawares. The madman then attacks with ferocity. This encounter only occurs once.

Berserker Cannibal CR 3
XP 800
HP 55 (Pathfinder Campaign Setting: Lands of the Linnorm Kings, "Berserker Cannibal")

12. **Owlbear.** The party encounters an **owlbear**. This horrific creature plows through trees and brush to get at its victims. A clever tracker that succeeds on a DC 10 Survival check can find its lair (a small cave). The lair contains the remains of a warrior along with the equipment they were wearing when they died — a suit of rusty full plate armor, a longsword, and 23 gp in a pouch.

Owlbear CR 4
XP 1,200
HP 47 (Pathfinder Roleplaying Game Bestiary, "Owlbear")

For random encounters in the swamp or near the river in the valley, roll on the table below and refer to the appropriate description after the table.

d12	Encounter
1	Fog
2-4	**Crocodile**
5	**Grey Ooze**
6	Quicksand
7	**Giant Beaver**
8-9	Herd of Animals
10	1d3 **Ghouls**
11	Giant Python
12	**Young Black Dragon**

1. Fog. Fog has settled in during the night. Being on watch consists of straining to see further than twenty feet in any direction because the area is heavily obscured. It seems the croak of frogs and the swish of passing crocodiles and snakes are just outside of your visible range. A sudden flurry of wings erupts a short distance from the camp, quickly followed by the frustrated cry of a swamp cougar. The swamp's nightlife seems to be happening all around you, but characters cannot see any of it.

2-4. Crocodile. A **crocodile** stalks the characters. It attacks any that enter the water (or automatically if it surprises any of the characters). If it kills someone, it grabs the body and retreats to deep water immediately.

Crocodile CR 2
XP 600
HP 22 (Pathfinder Roleplaying Game Bestiary, "Crocodile")

5. Grey Ooze. Anyone who has seen a blob movie knows how this one goes. The **grey ooze** retreats into the water if dropped to half health, otherwise it attacks mindlessly.

Gray Ooze CR 4
XP 1,200
HP 50 (Pathfinder Roleplaying Game Bestiary, "Gray Ooze")

6. Quicksand. Patches of quicksand present a deceptively solid appearance (appearing as undergrowth or open land) that might trap careless characters. A character approaching a patch of quicksand at a normal pace is entitled to a DC 8 Survival check to spot the danger before stepping in, but charging or running characters don't have a chance to detect a hidden patch before blundering into it. A typical patch of quicksand is 20 feet in diameter; the momentum of a charging or running character carries him 1d2 × 5 feet into the quicksand.

Effects of Quicksand: Characters in quicksand must make a DC 10 Swim check every round to simply tread water in place, or a DC 15 Swim check to move 5 feet in whatever direction is desired. If a trapped character fails this check by 5 or more, he sinks below the surface and begins to drown whenever he can no longer hold his breath (see the Swim skill description in Using Skills).

Characters below the surface of quicksand may swim back to the surface with a successful Swim check (DC 15, +1 per consecutive round of being under the surface).

Rescue: Pulling out a character trapped in quicksand can be difficult. A rescuer needs a branch, spear haft, rope, or similar tool that enables him to reach the victim with one end of it. Then he must make a DC 15 Strength check to successfully pull the victim, and the victim must make a DC 10 Strength check to hold onto the branch, pole, or rope. If both checks succeed, the victim is pulled 5 feet closer to safety. If the victim fails to hold on, he must make a DC 15 Swim check immediately to stay above the surface.

7. Giant Beaver. This large animal is not dangerous as long as they are left alone. Encounters can range from having the characters "trespass" on the beaver's territory (and dam) to randomly encountering one chewing down a tree. If the characters back off, the **giant beaver** will do the same. Beavers are territorial; however, if anyone can *speak with animals*, they can be friendly to a group as long as no threat is perceived. The safety of a giant beaver dam could be a wonderful hiding spot/campsite if the beaver is befriended or slain.

Giant Beaver CR 1
XP 400
HP 13 (Appendix, "Giant Beaver")

8-9. Herd of Animals. A herd of **deer** or otherwise innocuous beasts (**boar**, etc.) is spooked by the characters and runs by. Fast thinking players can shoot arrows and get a few free meals.

A crashing sound from the left greets you as a herd of animals burst from the thicket, spooked by your passage.

10. Ghouls. The party encounters 1d3 **ghouls**. These undead creatures are encountered mostly at night, although daytime encounters are possible. They haunt the swamp looking for flesh to eat; preferably human flesh.

Ghoul (1d3) CR 1
XP 400
HP 13 (Pathfinder Roleplaying Game Bestiary, "Ghoul")

11. Giant Python. Preying even on small crocodiles, the valley is home to large pythons (**giant constrictor snake**) that act as the local apex predator (excepting the dragon). These snakes typically do not attack anything during the day, preferring to sleep in the large trees that make up their nests. A typical encounter would be for a sleeping character to be attacked (surprised). Anyone bitten and squeezed while asleep cannot make a sound if they are dropped to 0 hit points. The snakes will typically retreat if wounded for more than half of their health.

Giant Constrictor Snake CR 5
XP 1,600
HP 59 (Pathfinder Roleplaying Game, "Advanced Giant Constrictor Snake")

12. Young Black Dragon. Living in the swamp is Recaltrix the **young black dragon**. She is a fine swimmer and prefers to come out of the swamp (posing as a crocodile) to flying (due to the heavy tree cover). Recaltrix is almost cat-like in her hunting techniques and prefers to watch her prey and attack when it suits her.

Recaltrix CR 7
XP 3,200
HP 76 (Pathfinder Roleplaying Game Bestiary, "Young Black Dragon")

KEYED ENCOUNTER AREAS

1. THE BLACK SPIRE

Ahead is a round, grassy mound with a slender finger of stone at its top. You can see the hill is about 20 feet high and 40 feet across at the base and the granite obelisk is 7 feet high.

Should someone climb the mound to examine the obelisk read the following:

The stone is old and weathered with an inscription at its base written in a forgotten script. Behind the obelisk is a large patch of freshly turned earth.

In the distance, the party will notice a tall, solitary black spire. Read the following:

Against the horizon is a tall, black spire. It stands about 15 feet tall, its surface beaten and cracked by weather. There are marks all over the surface, but too much time has passed since they were carved, and they are now just shallow tracings in the stone.

If the adventurers try to read the marks they will realize the carvings are in an ancient tongue that they cannot read. The obelisk is merely a border marker of an empire that fell long ago.

2. EMPTY ARMOR

Lying beside the road is a set of leather armor. A full torso of tiny leather plates sewn together lies on the grass, still in a round shape with the straps closed, so it gives the eerie impression of still being worn, even though the wearer cannot be seen.

The owner must have been a middle-sized man, quite broad-shouldered. If the area is searched, they find the leg armor scattered in the grass, dispelling the illusion that anyone is in the body armor. No helm, weapons pack or shoes can be found, only leather armor. The armor is still supple and soft, although in some places grass is growing up through it. Grass grows fast and leather weathers quickly, so this cannot have been here long.

3. THE BANDIT CAMP

There is an odd structure up ahead, instantly distinguished by straight lines in an environment where all things curve.

As the characters near the structure they can determine that it is the wall of an old building. Two sides still stand but the grassland has reclaimed all the area around the walls. The two walls, only a story high, are at right angles to each other and protrude awkwardly out of the plain. On the one facing you, part of the interior when the building was complete, you are struck by reflections off an old mosaic that covers the wall. The tiles are still bright blue and white. Despite the gaps from missing tiles, you recognize the scene as a mountain above a blue lake. No real mountains or lakes are visible anywhere. Living here are 3 **bandits**, there is a 50% chance that one is on guard and could spot the party at a distance. If the party is spotted, the bandits have time to setup an ambush and surprise the characters.

The bandits will not openly engage a larger party if they have surprise, but instead spread out in the brush and attack from all sides with missiles, targeting lightly armored foes first. They run if one of them is slain.

Bandit (3) CR ½
XP 200
HP 11 (Pathfinder Roleplaying Game GameMastery Guide, "Bandit")

Treasure. In the camp are 4 boxes of foodstuffs (20 days rations), a small keg of wine (worth 10 gp), bedrolls, a tinderbox, 4 flasks of lamp oil and a lantern. A sack of 60 tallow candles hangs from a hook on one wall. In one bedroll is a pouch containing a set of dice and 36 sp. Stretched between two poles are the partially tanned hides of three deer and a beaver (worth 1 gp each for the deer hides and 4 gp for the beaver pelt). Wedged into one of the poles is a hide scraper (worth 2 gp), and at the base is a pot of oily wax (worth 10 sp) used in tanning hides. A pile of firewood rests against another wall, and a chopping axe lays on top of it.

4. AN EMPTY BURROW

If any of the characters in the party pass a DC 12 Perception check, read the following.

Concealed amongst the tall grass is a large, flat boulder. Below the front edge someone or something has burrowed under the rock, creating a small shelter. The burrow is small and dark, but big enough for a person of average size to squeeze inside.

If someone looks inside, or enters, the small space is damp and smells strongly of wet fur. There are scatterings of bird bones and small piles of dried dung littering the floor. There is no other life in here except for a few beetles, crawling slowly along the wall. A ceramic drinking mug decorated with a rose quartz (worth 11 gp) is filled with torn paper and lies on its side on the floor. Mixed in the dirt near the mug is an assortment of 25 silver temple coins, stamped with the faces of saints (despite being silver, these are worth 25 gp total). At the bottom of the mug, is a golden sphere the size of a die (worth 15 gp). The wadded torn up fragments of paper each bear strange writing in deep indigo ink. This is the remains of a scroll of the spell *suggestion*. Amazingly, none of the tears broke any of the lettering, so if the scroll is repaired, or if the pieces are carefully laid out, it can still be used.

5. FOR THE WANT OF AN AXLE...

Nestled in the tall grass is a broken-down wagon. The peeling paint on the wind-blasted sideboards reads "Mygos' Traveling Mystical Emporium." The rear axle is broken, causing the wagon to sag drunkenly to the left. The leather harnesses are rotting away but are still connected to the shaft, but the tattered canvas cover has been destroyed leaving the metal frame highlighted against the sky like the ribs of some great beast. The wheels are sunk into the ground several inches.

It would seem that the wagon was abandoned long ago. A heavy woolen cloak, dyed dark blue, lies crumpled in a corner. Lighter blue ink has been used to trace wandering spiral patterns on the cloak, and the fine garment's edges have been trimmed in bone-white thread and feathers. A silver clasp in the shape of a walrus is used to secure the cloak (worth 36 gp). The right interior pocket holds a leather scroll case. Within the leather scroll case are three sheets of plain parchment scribed in a utilitarian, easy-to-read script. Each sheet is labeled "Protection for the Traveling Wizard" in the Common tongue. Each of the scrolls has a single cast of the *shield* spell. The thick leather scroll case has been repeatedly treated with waterproof and flame proofing oils. It weighs one pound and is worth 50 gp.

6. The Ogre Cave

If encountered during the day, read the following:

> A dim light can be seen coming from a cave entrance on the side of a steep cliff.

If encountered at night, read the following:

> There are several dozen bones and skulls littering the area at the base of the cliff. You notice what appears to be a cave entrance, somewhat hidden by brown, dead vegetation clinging to the cliff face.

The cave itself sits on the edge of a 40-foot cliff along the trail winding down into the valley. The trail itself is approximately 20 feet wide, with a sand-crumbly edge being held together by vegetation. The entrance is 10 feet wide and 7 feet high and is obscured with brambles and vines tacked onto a crossbar set of tree limbs. The vines are dead (unlike the rest of the vegetation on the hillside), and any character that passes a DC 10 Perception check will notice that this is probably a (poorly) concealed door.

The concealed door (the wood and vines) has 4 large brass bells on the back side that are hung to clink and ring with a considerable echo if the door is handled roughly. A successful DC 12 Perception check and careful examination of the false door reveals the bells and can prevent the ogre and his pet bear from immediately knowing they have company.

Beyond the door is a cave tunnel that is 20 feet wide and 12 feet high, branching of to the left and right sides at the 30-foot mark. The floor of the cave is course, tan sand, and broken stalactites and stalagmites litter the floor. A successful DC 10 Survival check indicates the stalactites and stalagmites were broken intentionally. Remains of a campfire freshly doused with water (daytime) or a small coal fire (at night) is immediately inside the doorway.

6A. The Pantry and Spring

> Hanging from the walls of the cave are three gutted deer, one stretched wolf pelt, and one dead (and gutted and dressed) human. Blood stains the sand near the hanging corpses, and flies and small cave beetles have been attracted to the remains.
>
> There is also a small pool of clean, clear water in the cave formed by flowing water from the cracks in the cave wall. Many small, blind crayfish move around the pool.

The left tunnel leads to a 40-foot diameter dead-end cave containing a 10-foot diameter pool of clean, clear water. The pool is 8 feet deep and flows through cracks in the walls of the pool in both directions, providing an excellent and replenishing water source.

Note. If the bell trap was sounded, and the characters went this way first, it is highly likely that they are attacked from the rear within 1 minute.

6B. The Ogre's Den

> The cave smells foul, like sweat and filth of some sort. There is a large pile of rubble that lines the back wall of the cave and huge pile of firewood is stacked against the left wall. A fire pit made of stacked rocks rests in the center of the cave, complete with a cooking spit and a large pot.

The right tunnel leads back 80 feet to a 50-foot-long, 30-foot-wide chamber. The ceiling is fully 12 feet high and has had all the lime deposits knocked down (the ogre was tired of hitting his head on them) and are piled along the back wall obscuring the ogre's nest (see below). The ceiling is well ventilated, and bats flitter about the roof entering and exiting the cave via small cracks in the roof.

Unless the players have been very stealthy, the **ogre** and his pet **black bear** are here and ready for combat. They fight to the death if encountered in the cave. If any of the characters speaks giant, it is also possible to parley with the ogre, although it thinks of any intrusion into its home as burglary and is therefore a very poor starting point for the negotiations. The pair will not pursue a large group outside of the cave.

Ogre CR 3
XP 800
HP 30 (Pathfinder Roleplaying Game Bestiary, "Ogre")

Black Bear CR 3
XP 800
HP 32 (Pathfinder Roleplllaying Game Bestiary, "Bear, Black")

The ogre's nest is a foul collection of torn bedding and soiled clothing, most of it shredded into long, worthless strips. The hilt of a greatsword pokes out from beneath the pile. It is in decent condition, if a bit rusty. Next to the sword is a suit of worn but serviceable scale mail sized for a large human or half-orc. A few bones are still lying near the scale mail, and they show evidence of having been gnawed on. A backpack lies by the armor, and, like the bedding, it has been shredded to worthlessness. Its contents lie strewn throughout the pile. The remains of trail rations are mixed with a destroyed pile of rope and scraps from a canvas sack. Several dozen coins are scattered amongst the refuse (69 gp, 148 sp). Buried in the back is a shortbow which, surprisingly, shows no wear save a missing bowstring. A quiver of arrows is here as well, chewed through, but still containing three silver arrows.

Poison Needle Trap. Next to the bedding is a latched chest with a poison needle hidden within the lock. If the chest is opened without disarming the trap, the poison needle springs out 3 inches from the lock and delivers the poison dose.

Poison Latch Needle Trap CR 1
XP 400
Type mechanical; **Perception** DC 20; **Disable Device** DC 20
Trigger touch; **Reset** none
Effect Atk +5 melee (1 damage plus greenblood oil)

Greenblood Oil
Type poison (injury); **Save** Fortitude DC 13; **Frequency** 1/round for 4 rounds; **Cure** 1 save
Effect 1 Con damage

Treasure. The chest contains a light leather riding saddle worth 10 gp, a square of fine lace worth 5 gp, and a pair of white elbow-length gloves sprinkled with freshwater pearls around the top that will fetch 340 gp. Beside them, wrapped in a rag, is a stick of charcoal and a 3-inch diameter crystal sphere. At the bottom is a tall thin book with poorly executed carving on its wooden covers is half-full of amateur sketches of people and animals, done in charcoal (5 sp). Caught in a seam at the bottom is a red-brown garnet worth 100 gp.

Polished to a mirror-like sheen, the 3-inch diameter crystal sphere is surprisingly heavy and is about the size of a plum. The sphere is an *ioun torch* and erupts in bright silver light that clearly illuminates the area around.

Next to the chest is a bucket and a longbow made of yew with a grip of pale calfskin lies beside a quiver of deer hide tooled all over with cleverly intertwined hunting scenes. There are no arrows in the quiver, but it holds a silver flask (etched with flower decorations) which is full of rich red wine. The bow is worth 75 gp, the quiver is worth 15 gp, and the flask is worth 10 gp.

The heavy, solid brass bucket holds two fine silver platters worth 30 gp each, a black onyx cat with yellow citrines for eyes worth 250 gp, a hinged box with a tiny hunting scene on the top in bright enamels worth 15 gp, and a heavy coin pouch. The little box holds a fine powder (one-half pound cinnamon, or a spell component or other spice). In the coin pouch are 65 gp, 393 sp, 203 cp and 3 pieces of turquoise worth 10 gp each.

7. River Crossing

At the bottom of the deep, wide chasm before you is a rapidly flowing river that churns with white water as it flows between tall boulders and rough, sharp rocks. A large tree has been placed across the chasm to serve as the bridge.

The path is split by a deep chasm with a river at the bottom. There is a bridge across it, made of a single log. A big tree has been cut and dropped over the chasm. There is no other way across except to walk on the tree. The tree was more than a hundred feet tall and at least sixty of those feet are out over the chasm. Below is a river with rushing white water between tall boulders. The bark is still on this tree bridge, but the branches have been chopped off. A slightly lighter color down the center shows the path. It's about a foot wide and level. On both sides another six inches of log slopes away. It's not a difficult path, if you don't mind being suspended in space sixty feet above a wild river. Crossing the bridge safely requires a successful DC 8 Acrobatics check.

8. Ruined Cottage

The trail winds over a dark sandy soil, comfortable to walk or ride on because it gives slightly but makes little dust. The temperature is pleasant in the shade of the great trees. The air carries sweet plant scents.

You smell the pleasant, sweet scents of the forest, and the temperature is cool and comfortable in the shade of the tall trees that line the path. In all directions are tall broad-leafed trees reaching upward. Occasionally the trunk of a pine, leaking sticky, fragrant sap, is present among the other trees. Middle-sized shrubs dot the forest floor. Between them are ferns and grasses but most of the ground is bare except for fallen, brown leaves and fuzzy deep green mosses.

There is a ruined building ahead that stands in stark contrast to the verdant forest. Only one wall stands, but you can see a dark empty area where the interior was, and sections of the fallen walls are visible. In front weeds, rare here in the forest, form a wild tangle of green and brown shoots. It is both forlorn and ugly. Four transparent glass bottles are lined up side by side on a small shelf inside the remains.

Each glass bottle is large enough to hold roughly a pint of liquid and is stoppered by a substantial cork and are filled with a viscous liquid in which different items of food are packed. The first contains pickled garlic bulbs, the second pickled eggs of some sort, perhaps hens' eggs, the third, strands of red cabbage and the final one has small, silvery fish. In the bottom of the fish bottle are also 4 silvery temple coins (worth 40 gp).

9. Spiders and Flies

What began as the occasional spider web has now quickly blossomed into gossamer curtains and sheets of webbing. There is evidence that the webs have been hacked and burned away from the trail, but the forest has web upon web. All around is the smell dust and decay. Here and there, you see hanging objects that could be bodies; too many of them seem to be humanoid in shape. Everywhere you look, you see gleams that seem to be glittering eyes staring back at you. Eerily, you notice that you can no longer hear the normal sounds of the forest—only the gentle sighing of a mournful wind.

There are 8 **giant spiders** lurking in the trees. Each round 1d3-1 spiders notice the party and stalk them, attacking once 3 or more spiders have seen them.

Giant Spider (8) CR 1
XP 400
HP 16 (Pathfinder Roleplaying Game Bestiary, "Giant Spider")

Treasure. One of the corpses has a sack that contains a large, half-burned yellow candle, two thin gray woolen blankets, a heavy black skillet, an old, large wooden spoon, a mink pelt worth 20 gp, a rabbit pelt worth 2 gp, and a black leather belt, carefully made with inconspicuous, very fine tooling along its length. However, the buckle is missing and was very sloppily cut off. The sack also holds a coil of coarse hemp rope, a pair of gauntlets of heavy cowhide dyed black, held by solid iron rivets reworked to look like stars, and a silver key. Loose at the bottom are various coins totaling 7 gp, 19 sp, and 33 cp, and black and white stones — 2 pieces of obsidian worth 10 gp each, 1 small, fractured piece of onyx worth 20 gp, and 2 small, rough pieces of quartz worth 10 gp each.

Also present is a club hewn from a gnarled oaken limb, preserved with a dark finish. The large burl of wood at the business end has been stained a dark, rusty red from repeated use. The grip is bound in strips of cream-colored leather bearing fine runes dyed into the material. The leather strips can be unwrapped from the club to reveal two castings of the druid spell *shillelagh*. Each strip is four inches wide and two feet long.

10. Mysterious Shrine

Next to the path but partially hidden by a screen of smaller plants is a small shrine. Characters who roll a DC 12 Perception check notice the shrine.

A small shrine composed of stacked rocks and twigs has been established around a crudely carved 3-foot statue. The statue has chubby arms and legs and a welcoming smile, together with some tiny clay bowls and plates. Bits of food and drink have been set in front of the god as a form of tribute. A small scorched area perhaps indicates where a fire has been set, although it may have been nothing more than a large candle.

11. A Fork in the Road

The ground surrounding the path here is completely blanketed with a vibrant, blue clover, the bright full blooms almost glowing in the gloom of the woods. Hovering and darting above the clover are tiny white butterflies. There is a rustling among the clover and a small green viper courses his way through the plants.

Careful inspection and a successful DC 12 Perception check reveals a glimpse of something gleaming dully among the greenery. If the adventurers search through the clover, they discover a small pewter skeleton key, the top of which is carved to resemble a squat little face of a mouse with a protruding tongue. There is a 10% chance that the little viper (**venomous snake**), which slithers quickly from the clover bed and across the path, is disturbed by the party and attacks.

Venomous Snake CR 1
XP 400
HP 13 (Pathfinder Roleplaying Game Bestiary, "Snake, Venomous")

MCMLXXV
Wilderness

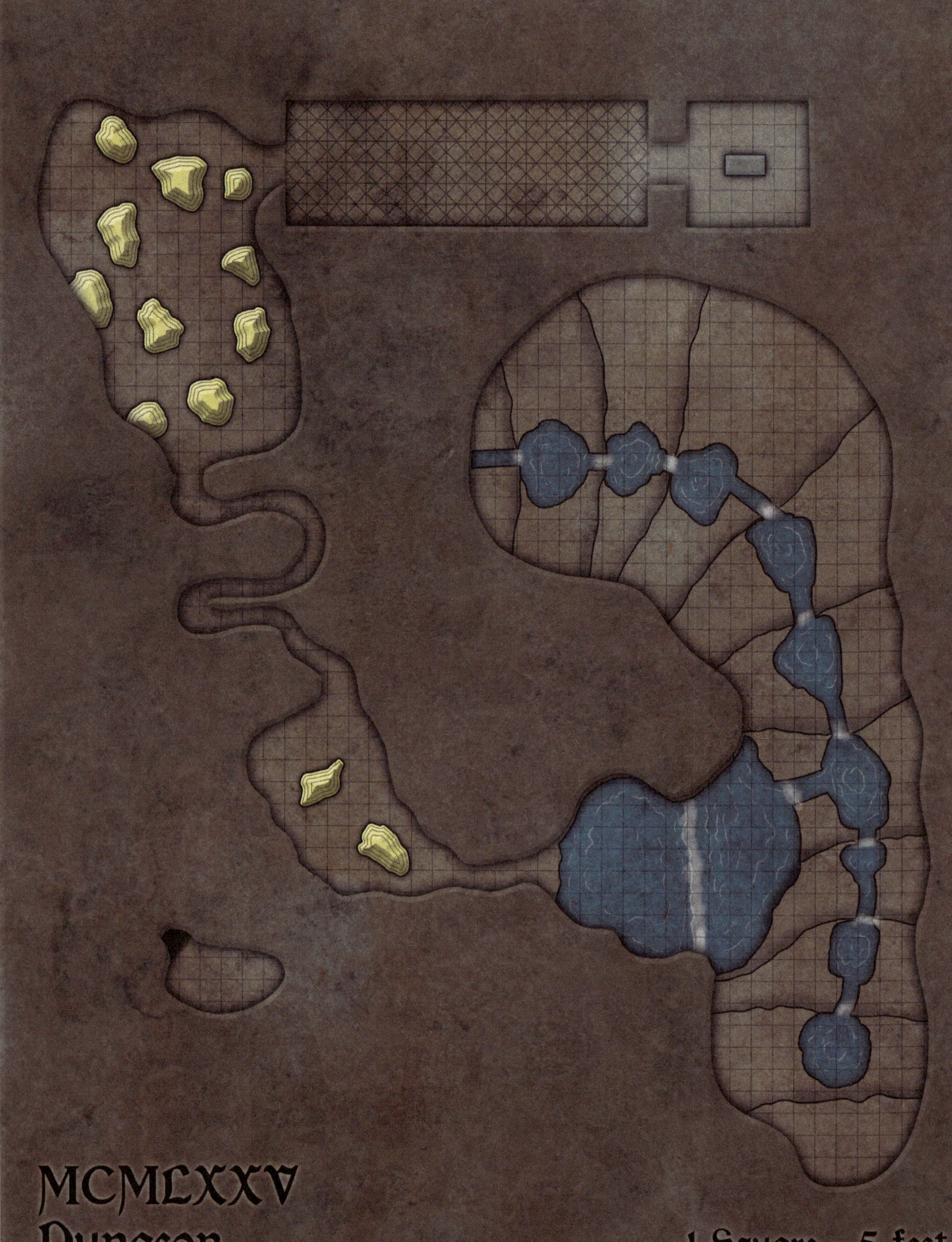

MCMLXXV
Dungeon
1 Square - 5 feet

MCMLXXV
Wilderness
Town
1
2
3
4
5
6
7
8
9
10
11
12
13
14
15
16
17
18
19
20
21
22
23
24
25
26
27
x

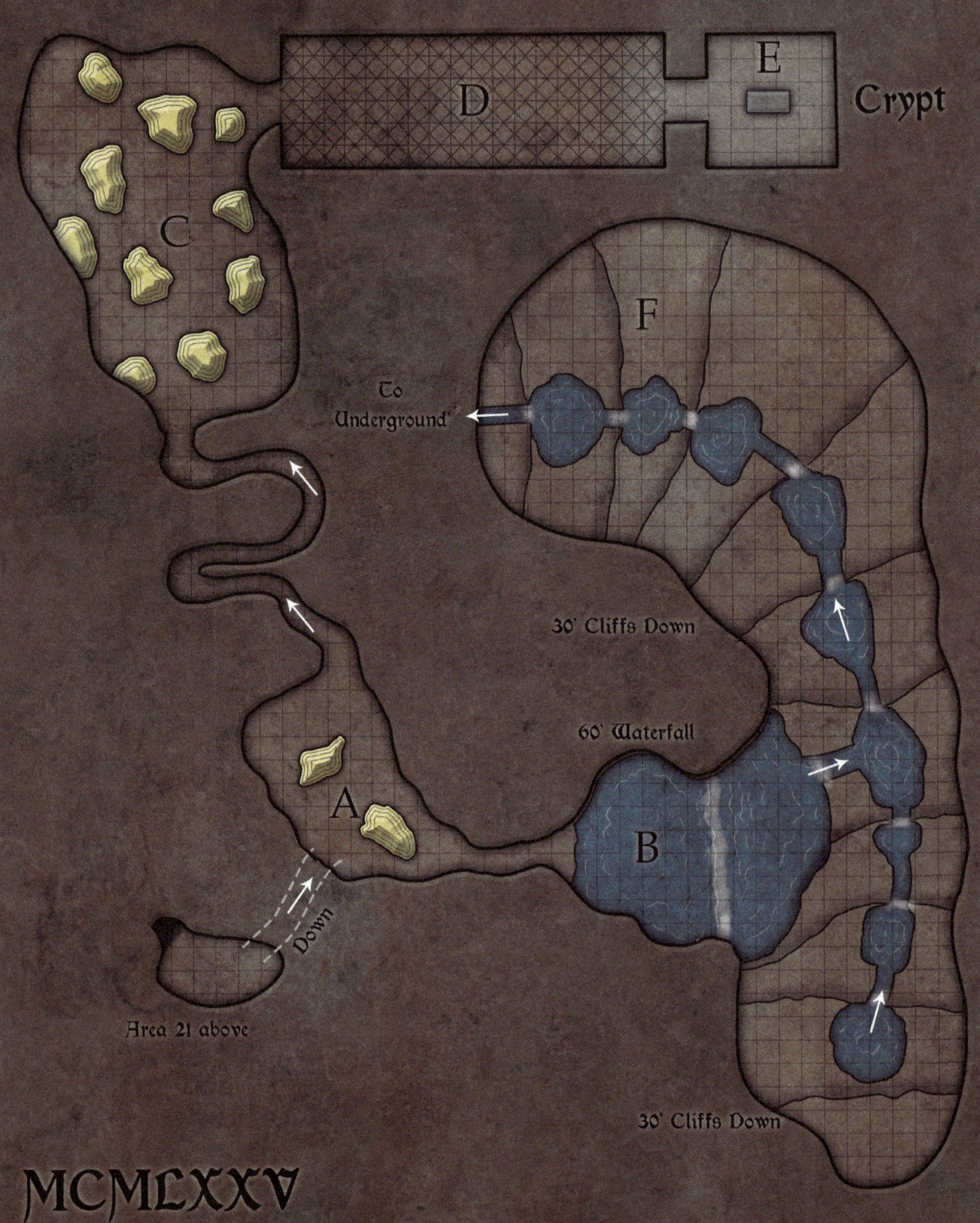

D
E
Crypt
C
F
To Underground
30' Cliffs Down
60' Waterfall
A
B
Down
Area 21 above
30' Cliffs Down
MCMLXXV
Dungeon
1 Square - 5 feet

Huge, ancient trees with massive trunks reach heights that you've rarely seen before. Twisted and tangled roots, some up to four feet high and many covered with dozens of tiny red mushrooms, cover the trail and make travel difficult and dangerous. Further down the trail, the roots of two of these forest behemoths have intertwined, forming a latticework wall that bars your path.

The trees are spaced much wider apart and more sunlight reaches the forest floor. Some of the trees are ancient, reaching heights of a hundred feet or more and spanning 10 to 15 feet across. The many tree's great, twisted roots have grown over the trail in many places, at times rising four feet above the ground before delving back into the loamy earth. Dozens of tiny red mushrooms sprout from the soft wood of the roots, creating a strange almost anthill-like appearance. Along in the trail, two of the enormous trees have grown toward each other, their great roots intertwining and forming a latticework wall that completely bars the path.

At the blocked section, the roots have grown in a way that suggests a ladder, easy to climb despite the slippery nature of the moss and the mushrooms growing on them. The roots go up about eight feet. If any of the party wish to climb them, they will need to succeed on a DC 10 Climb check. As they climb, they find a small "nest" of twigs and leaves tucked up against the trunk of one great tree. It is about the right size for a creature that is roughly two feet tall. It contains a dirty suit of clothes in a very small size, a tiny pair of shoes, and a small locked iron box. If any of the party has the skeleton key above, it will fit into the keyhole and can be used to unlock the box, otherwise a successful DC 15 Disable Device check will be sufficient to open the lock. Inside are arrayed rows of fish hooks in different sizes and materials. The smallest would be suitable for landing minnows while some of the larger ones would probably be strong enough to cope with a particularly fierce shark. Some of the smaller hooks are fashioned from stone and some kind of crystal, while the larger ones are made from some kind of steel. There is a total of 80 hooks. If anyone steals the hooks, **Jasper the Leprechaun**, who owns them will become very upset.

The little fellow hides invisibly high in a tree and does not bother the party unless his abode is disturbed. Should the group leave food (or wine), Jasper might be favorably disposed towards them, even helping them in their next fight, although he still will not reveal himself. If the hooks are stolen by the party, the opposite is true. He will instead use his major image spell-like ability to create illusions of additional enemies when the group is in combat and will plague the group with untied shoelaces, spoiled food, and misplaced items. You can use your imagination to create havoc as desired.

If a great quantity of wine or spirits is left as an offering, the party has an opportunity to capture Jasper. Like all his kind, he has a propensity to indulge a bit heavily when given the opportunity. While he remains invisible, the drunk leprechaun can be located by his loud snoring. If captured, Jasper offers his pot of 400 gold pieces for his freedom. The gold is buried on a small hill not far from the tree lattice.

Jasper the Leprechaun   CR 3
XP 800
HP 24 (Appendix, "Jasper the Leprechaun")

At the edge of a thickly forested territory, you can only marvel at the new plant life all around. As you take in nature, you feel water begin to seep into your boots.

Anyone looking down notices that the forest floor ahead is flooded as it slowly becomes a soggy morass. The swamp ahead is alive with new growth such as yellow birch trees with new catkins flowers hanging from the branches and the dark green scale-like leaves of white cedar trees. Any character that succeeds on a DC 13 KNowledge (Nature) check can identify the different trees and flowers that grow throughout the swamp.

They also notice the intense smells all around, most of which can be identified by a character that succeeds on a DC 12 Perception check and a DC 10 Knowledge (Nature) check. Some enticing aromas come from new flowers blooming above the water, but others are not so appealing, like the smell of fetid leaves still decaying from last year's fall season. One cannot see very far ahead into the swamp due to the overgrowth of the trees that make the area heavily obscured.

Wet Feet

The path descends into the dark waters of the swamp. Tall grasses grow up in the shallows where the path should be, and sections of the trail are underwater. The murky waters swirl sluggishly and ripples indicate something large swimming across the road just below the surface. Ahead the path rises out of the water and continues on.

If the adventurers follow the path they will find that the water covering it is waist deep. Anyone who does not succeed on a DC 10 Reflex saving throw slips and falls. You should decide if there is a risk of an encounter. Also, if the adventurers move to the right or left of the road the water quickly rises to neck deep.

A plump, insolent-looking rat sits, smirking, on the matted moss on top of a dead stump in the water at the side of the trail and licks its lips suggestively, daring anyone to throw a stone at it. Long white whiskers stand out against its grey, well-groomed fur, its green eyes gleaming in what remains of the daylight. Its eyes betray an intelligence far greater than any rat should have. A burst of foul-smelling gas suddenly fills the air as the water around the stump bubbles.

Rat CR ¼
XP 100
HP 4 (Pathfinder Roleplaying Game Bestiary, "Rat")

If attacked, the **rat** can easily be slain. A better idea would be to toss it something shiny.

The rat's nest is a few yards into the swamp, just off the trail. In its nest are several items. For some reason, this rat feels a need to "trade" shiny objects from time to time. Should the characters toss it an object, it runs off and returns with an exchange gift. It will do this up to three times. What the rat brings back is randomly determined, but can include:

d8	Trade Item
1	A silver piece
2	A gold piece
3	A small gem (10 gp)
4	A worthless polished rock
5	A broken piece of china or glass
6	A large white tooth (of a crocodile or other beast)
7	A small mirror made of silver (15 gp)
8	A magical *ring of protection +1*

Items 7 and 8 can only be gotten once.

15. Bubble Spit and Chomp

The swamp bubbles and spits, methane deposits just under the water exploding rhythmically. The air is so humid and close that it's hard to breathe.

There is a **crocodile** on the opposite shore, resting, after having eaten recently. It will attack if someone enters the water, attempting to surprise the unsuspecting individual. If the party comes back this way again, the crocodile may be hungry (50% chance) and lying in ambush near the water's edge.

Crocodile CR 2
XP 600
HP 22 (Pathfinder Roleplaying Game Bestiary, "Crocodile")

16. Just Chomp

Here the swamp forest forms a gallery overhead. Great trees with air plants dangling from them arch over the swamp. The water is so still one can see their reflection in its dark surface. The tree trunks are gray or occasionally light brown, thin and smooth. Most are quite plain, but a few are twisted round and round with climbing vines. They branch far overhead, but the limbs are long and bend down to dip leaves in the water. A bright red and white butterfly basks on an olive-green leaf near the water's edge, its wings flicking slowly up and down.

Another **crocodile**, hungry and on the hunt, lies in wait in the tall reeds at the water's edge. It attacks anyone within 10 feet of the edge of the trail.

Crocodile CR 2
XP 600
HP 22 (Pathfinder Roleplaying Game Bestiary, "Crocodile")

17. The Island of Screams

This portion of the bog smells of rot, decay, and fermenting wood. Every place where the ground rises out of the water is speckled with tiny white and tan mushrooms. Fallen logs lay soaked and decomposing all around, most of them covered with broader, slimy looking fungus and moss.

A 40-foot diameter island rises out of the swamp, but to get there, the party must move through 30 feet of chest deep water.

The trees on the island that are still standing are ringed with brown shelf-like fungi in tiers around their trunks. The mushrooms are getting larger the further onto the island. I the center of the island is a small area where they seem to have replaced the trees entirely. About a half-dozen of the fungi are tall enough for the caps to spread above the character's heads and there is a fine mist of yellowish green spores sprinkling down from each. Beyond these large mushrooms, the other mushrooms gradually get smaller again. These large mushrooms include 3 **shriekers**, which will emit an audible shriek if a creature comes too close.

If the shriekers are disturbed, the sound draws the attention of a **troll** that lairs nearby.

Shrieker CR –
XP –

This human-sized purple mushroom emits a piercing sound that lasts for 1d3 rounds whenever there is movement or a light source within 10 feet. This shriek makes it impossible to hear any other sound within 50 feet. The sound attracts nearby creatures that are disposed to investigate it. Some creatures that live near shriekers learn that this noise means there is food or an intruder nearby.

Troll CR 5
XP 1,600
HP 63 (Pathfinder Roleplaying Game Bestiary, "Troll")

Treasure. The troll carries a large heavy sack contains a length of fine brown silk (3 yards), a plain gold cup too small for a halfling to get a good drink (worth 25 gp), and a large piece of carved white rock. The carving is two hands long and is the head of a man with an aquiline nose and thinning hair. It was obviously broken off from a larger sculpture. Also in the sack is an iron mace studded with pointed spikes longer than a finger. A ball of thick white yarn has become tangled around the mace and its spikes. There is also a small shiny round metal cylinder with a cap that holds toothpicks. At the bottom of the sack is 19 sp, 25 cp, and 2 pale blue gems (quartz, worth 10 gp each).

18. A Really Big Tree

A massive tree, large enough that if a group of six held hands they would likely not be able to reach around its base, stands before you. The bark is weathered and dark with age and odd cracks and crevices. Rich, red-brown wood can be seen where the bark has come off the tree. Along the trail, the great tree is on land, but the other side of its massive trunk is green swamp water. Its limbs, many of which are larger than most trees, spread wide and far overhead, shading the area.

At the base of the tree you can see a forest altar of some kind, adorned by fresh flowers that have been layered on older dry flowers and other unidentifiable offerings.

Beyond the tree is a large granite boulder the size of a small mountain. The path snakes around the boulder and opens upon a colorful field full of vibrant flowers of every shape and size that sway with the wind. Floral scents fill your nostrils as does the tickling itch of pollen. The soft echoes of a nearby stream leave you feeling serene and calm, relieved to have escaped the swamp.

It appears initially that the party has exited the swamp, but another step forward proves this wrong, as feet submerge into the cold and moisture inundated soil. This is a rare find indeed, as normally flowers like the ones mentioned above do not grow in swamps. There may be a special reason behind this — it is possible that a swamp druid resides here or perhaps the soil here is just perfect for this type of plant life.

Not far ahead, thick vines that give off a pungent odor grow out of deep cracks in the head of an ancient statute. Much taller than a man, the statue no longer stands, rather it is partially submerged in the oily muck, leaving only part of its nose and snarling mouth visible above the scum of dead leaves and still water.

A DC 12 Perception check indicates that the statue must have once been painted striking greens and yellows and reds, but age has reduced its brilliant colors to pastels. Upon closer inspection, it appears that the head has been severed, and the roots of a twisted river oak grow in thick tangles around it.

Some distance away lies an enormous stone hand, missing half its fingers.

The hand is the home to a nest of 12 water moccasins (**venomous snakes**). The snakes are highly aggressive, and attack if disturbed, with 1d4 of them joining combat each round until all are slain or the characters retreat more than 60 feet from the statue. Of the rest of the forgotten statue, there is no sign.

Venomous Snake (12) CR 1
XP 400
HP 13 (Pathfinder Roleplaying Game Bestiary, "Snake, Venomous")

19. THE POND

The trail vanishes into a pond here. As you skirt the edge of the pond looking for the trail, branches slap at your face, while your gear gets caught by grasping vines.

The pond appears to be at least 100 feet across, but its edge is irregular and not easy to see. At the far edge, at what ought to be the pond's exit, is a beaver dam. The dam is woven of logs, sticks and leaves, and is easily 6 feet higher than the stream at its center and at least 3 feet higher at its edges. It is in excellent repair, and some of the branches on it still have green leaves. The pond spreads out from there and the top of a beaver lodge can be seen 20 yards out in the pond. The stream spills under the dam, filling a wide channel. Because the pond covers the trail, the players have to pick a place to ford the stream, either above or below the dam. The trail continues once the pond is crossed or the stream is forded. Curiously, there is no beaver.

Several small turtles can be seen bunched together on a log a dozen yards from the edge of the pond and around the beaver lodge. They bask in the occasional beam of sunlight.

All of the turtles seem to be in a strange posture with their heads and legs sticking stiffly out from their shells.

A giant turtle (uses **crocodile** statistics) hides in the pond. Anyone at the ponds edge for more than 3 rounds will likely be surprised and attacked. It will attempt to surprise anyone that wanders into the water and will attack while submerged.

Giant Turtle CR 2
XP 600
HP 22 (Pathfinder Roleplaying Game Bestiary, "Crocodile")

20. NARROW PATH, BIG PIG

The path follows a stream for a bit and then rises out of the mud a several feet, creating a ledge down to the water. Although the trail is clear, and the banks of the stream are obvious, the plants that grow along the edge of the stream are very dense and difficult to move through.

The distance from the ledge to the water is about 8 feet.

Along the ridge, a female **dire boar** noses for grubs before a gently swaying wall of cattails. Six piglets nose along the ground, their snouts and stubby, immature tusks covered in rich brown mud. They oink happily, till the mother catches sight of the party. She stands her ground, grunting angrily, as her young barrel into the thicket. As soon as they are out of sight, she joins them, knocking over cattails in her haste to get to safety. If the group does not retreat in 3 rounds, she attacks. The only way around her is to swim or wade through the water below.

Dire Boar CR 4
XP 1,200
HP 42 (Pathfinder Roleplaying Game Bestiary, "Boar, Dire")

21. ST. ELMO

The terrain that the party must move across is considered difficult. Each step they take results in the mud creating a suction (with accompanying sound) forcing the characters to exert themselves to move the short distance. Furthermore, there is quicksand in the area. Any character that fails on a DC 8 Perception check could find themselves waist deep in quicksand before they know it.

You can see an unusually large tree ahead. It is vacant of all its leaves, and its branches reach out like arms in towards the group. The dark gray lines that run vertically through its pasty white trunk seem to form a face. A large knot protruding from the center of the tree resembles a nose, while a hollowed opening under the knot resembles a mouth. A slowly pulsating, yellowish light escapes the "mouth", much like that of a firefly in the distance and dances off into the trees.

The glowing light in the center of the tree is a highly dangerous **will-o'-wisp** and is far beyond the abilities of the group. It will not attack unless attacked, but instead will try to draw the group into a nearby patch of quicksand. If the characters are not drowned, the wisp heads off in search of other victims.

Will-o'-wisp CR 6
XP 2,400
HP 40 (Pathfinder Roleplaying Game Bestiary, "Will-o'-wisp")

22. BOBBLEHEAD

A curiously-shaped object that resembles a white stone catches your attention as it bobs just beneath the surface of the water.

The bobbing object is an elongated skull. The skin has withered away, and a few tendons have been exposed, as has the bone. The jaw bone is particularly prominent, much more so than any other skull the characters have seen in a life of adventuring. A few wisps of hair cling to its pate. A copper coin appears to have been pushed into its empty mouth. The coin is very old and unidentifiable, while the skull has in fact been mummified by the effects produced by the swamp. Extensive digging would ultimately reveal the rest of the skeleton but would also cause a significant cave-in of the submerged branches and vegetable matter on which the adventurers walk.

23. THE END IS NEAR!

The hanging moss and drooping tree branches part to reveal a small clearing next to a slowly moving stream of clear water. You can hear the sound of the water moving as it swirls past a small statue of a man in the stream channel. Fashioned from dark marble, the figure is carved with an ornate suit of armor, sword and shield. Lichen and moss cling to its base, swayed by the motion of the water rippling flowing past.

Even a few golden fish can be seen swimming beneath the sunlight dappled surface as the birds sing a cheerful song above. This seems to be the only place in the swamp-land where the choking torrents of green slime and brackish water do not touch, as if it's protected by magic or another force—even the air smells fresher.

If the party follows the stream channel path, they reach the edge of the swamp and head up out of it. The trail turns gravelly and the land seems solid, no longer waterlogged. The smells are much less intense, and the humidity drops noticeably. Overhead the trees thin and the sun beats down. Bird songs are fewer and more distant. Pink and purple flowers are small and hidden on the ground amid thin, pale green leaves. A few of the biting flies follow for several dozen paces, but then they too are gone. Only the mud remains, drying into a hard shell on legs and into stiff blotches everywhere else it splattered. Of course, someone might find a leech sucking on their leg later in the day. The forest ahead is sparsely populated by very large trees and huge granite boulders, creating a maze-like atmosphere.

24. TREES AND ROCKS

The trail emerges from the rocks and forest into a glade. The path, which has been clear through the trees, vanishes under the vibrant plants of the meadow. Long slender blades of various grasses cover the ground. The area where the trail leaves the meadow on the other side can be seen, leading uphill.

The path up the rocky ground under the trees 100 yards away is obvious even from this distance. A straight line to the path will have the characters stepping on buttercups and iris, pushing bright flowers into the soft ground. It is squishy underfoot and water oozes into their footprints. At the center of the meadow, the area is flooded, with a few inches of water flowing over everything.

The low hill just ahead is topped by a badly misshapen tree. It looks as if the tree has experienced some horrible accident.

It is split down the middle; each half now hangs out from the base of the trunk as if the tree was struck with a giant axe. Closer examination reveals obvious charring along the bark and the interior wood. The smell of burnt wood is evident but has faded into a faint tinge in the air. The lightning that destroyed this tree did so months ago.

A few feet beyond the tree is a large rock that is covered with crude writing.

The large, moss-covered rock stands ten feet in height, directly ahead in the center of the path. The path goes around it on each side. Drawn in tree sap on the surface of the rock is an arrow pointing down. If the party looks closer and one of the characters succeed on a DC 8 Perception check, they will notice that at the base of the rock, buried in the dark soil, is a roll of soft tree bark, that tied with string like a scroll. Unrolling the crude bark scroll reveals several crude depictions of orcs scratched into the surface of the bark.

25. GOBLINS!

In the distance you can barely make out what looks like an old, ruined building of some sort sitting on top of the next hill.

Closer examination reveals that the building is a ruined temple of some sort, and from the look of things, it has been abandoned for dozens of years. Only part of one wall remains, standing grimly over the rubble strewn around the site. A single stone staircase leads six or seven feet into the air, ending at nothing. Planks and timbers stick up from the ruin randomly. The entire site is strewn with stones that vary in size from pebbles to blocks too large for anyone to lift. This ruined building is the home of 4 **goblins**, a **goblin leader**, and a **goblin shaman**. There is a 50% chance during the day that they are not on guard (they fell asleep) and can be surprised. Otherwise, they have an alert guard and actively attempt to surprise the party.

Goblin (4) CR 1/3
XP 135
HP 6 (Pathfinder Roleplaying Game Bestiary, "Goblin")

Goblin Leader CR 3
XP 800
HP 20 (Appendix, "Goblin Leader")

Goblin Shaman CR 3
XP 800
HP 33 (Pathfinder 1: Burnt Offerings, "Goblin Druid 4")

Treasure. If the characters loot the goblins, they gain the following treasures:
*A dagger with an ornate, gilded hilt studded with blue and red gemstones (spinels) and embossed in arabesque patterns (150 gp). The blade is curved almost back to the hilt and has fine writing engraved along the back of the blade on either side. The writing is recognizable as that of an ancient desert-dwelling people with a successful DC 18 Knowledge (History) check. The actual meaning of the inscription has been lost to time.
*Rough bone dice carved from cow bone and stored in a leather pouch (5 gp).
*A small white ceramic container sealed with a silver-embossed glass screw-on cap, inside which is a creamy white salve flecked with crushed herbs, bearing a strong, pleasant aroma of lanolin and thyme. The beauty salve heals minor superficial wounds and blemishes, instantly curing acne, boils, rashes, cuts, and similar lesions. There are 12 applications of the salve remaining in the jar.

Inside the goblin lair is an old wooden chest. The large wooden chest crumbles and falls apart as it opens, the wood having rotted over years of sitting in this place.
Treasure. Anyone sorting through the old wood and dust while succeeding on a DC 11 Perception check, finds a sleeveless leather tunic of such thin leather that it would provide no protection against attack, but it is decorated nicely and in good condition. Lifting the tunic reveals something is stored within it. Inside is a hinged metal box about a hand wide, a finger tall, and a palm deep, that contains several coins (14 gp, 11 sp), and a small figurine fashioned in gold of an elf maiden sitting on her knees, looking down as if in meditation (62 gp).

26. ANOTHER POND

Beyond the ruined temple, the terrain is strewn with rocks and occupied by huge trees. You hear the sound of running water.

If one of the characters succeeds on a DC 10 Perception check while following the sounds of the water for another fifty yards, the sound will continue to become more distinct.

Obscured by a particularly large tree is a large pool of water, big enough to be called a pond but too small to describe as a lake. A stream is feeding the pond on the opposite side from where you stand. It seems odd that although the gurgling rivulet is running into the pool of water, there is no stream running out.

Intelligent players will realize that water must be leaving the pond from somewhere, or else it would continuously rise and flood the area, which doesn't seem to be happening. There must be an egress below the surface of the water where the overflow makes its way underground to some unknown destination. You may decide that the hidden waterway pathway leads to an underground cavern or all the way to another stream that resurfaces elsewhere.

To notice the cavern at the bottom of the pool, a character must succeed on a DC 12 Perception check. If the check is successful, read:

As you peer into the clear depths of the pond it is difficult to tell how deep the pool actually goes, but you can just make out a dark shape that looks like it might be a cave.

The pond is about thirty feet deep and the cavern that leads underground is at the bottom. The water if fresh and safe to drink.

27. X MARKS THE SPOT

Past the pond and down into some thick rocks is where the map indicated that the "treasure" exists.

After passing through some thick undergrowth, you come upon a wide circular clearing. Around the edge of the clearing is a ring of menhirs, each about ten feet tall and situated a few paces from the surrounding trees. The ground between the stones is an overgrown mix of clover, wildflowers and stunted berry bushes—except in the center of the clearing, which is dominated by a massive slab of weathered stone, fully as wide and long as a hay wagon. The stone sits atop a mound of earth, and a circle of ground around it has been cleared down to the dirt in the recent past. The slab itself has been tipped halfway off the mound, as if someone tried to knock it from its perch. You can see that the surface is covered in dark stains.

A character that succeeds on a DC 12 Perception check and searches the area beyond the standing stones will find there is a small, 4-foot diameter cave entrance that is hidden behind a small copse of trees. The cave leads to a small dungeon complex below.

Your torchlight reveals that the walls of the cave have intricate stone etchings and highly detailed cave paintings on them. The frescoes depict warfare, hunting, and even marriage rituals. As you walk through the cavern, bone fragments mixed with sand and gravel crunches beneath your feet.

No one has entered this cave for hundreds of years, and it was completely hidden until a recent landslide exposed the tunnel entrance to the outside. The entrance opens into a 30-foot long, 15-foot wide passage that ends at a sinkhole.

At the end of the passage is a sinkhole that abruptly descends deep into the bowels of the earth. Warm air flows from the depths of the hole.

Climbing down into the hole is a slow and potentially treacherous task, requiring a successful DC 12 Climb check to descend.

THE DUNGEON

This small cave complex is the treasure trove indicated on the map. The dungeon itself has several offshoot tunnels lead to unmapped (and unwritten) areas, which can all be used to expand the dungeon. You can add your own chambers and encounters to this area and it can act as a starting point for an extended dungeon adventure. As written, no wandering monsters are present here, however, if additional encounters are desired, they can certainly be added.

The cave complex contains a couple of very dangerous encounters and an ancient tomb. The traps laid by the creators of the complex are old, and often fail to function. The mechanical traps in area D (as noted in that section) are particularly affected, although the other physical hazards (and pits) still function normally.

A. THE ENTRANCE

The shaft from the sinkhole opens into a chamber with tunnels leading out of it on the left and the right. The walls and floor are damp and drops of water rain down sporadically from the ceiling, draining into the loose gravel floor. Bats flit about above, and guano covers the rocks and stalactites below. The floor itself is relatively even, sloping only slightly to the left.

The chamber is 30 feet wide. Each tunnel entrance is roughly 5 feet wide and 7 feet high. The right tunnel appears dry and leads to area C, while a tiny rivulet of drainage runs down the left tunnel to area B.

B. THE WET CAVE

The tunnel opens before you into a large cave with a low ceiling. The stone walls are stained with iron bacteria and the cave itself is filled with orange-colored water. The water cascades out of the far side of the entrance, creating a small waterfall. The falling water echoes as it splashes far below.

The tunnel opens into a large cave that is 60-feet in diameter and has a low ceiling that is 8 feet high. The water in the cave is only 3 feet deep but it is hard to tell that without testing the depth or entering the water.

The waterfall drops 60 feet to area F. Anyone getting within 10 feet of the waterfall area must make a DC 8 Acrobatics check or slip and fall. If the check fails, the character must succeed on a DC 10 Reflex saving throw or be carried over the waterfall, sustaining 6d6 bludgeoning damage from the fall.

C. STONE RATS

The tunnel winds to the left and then back to the right, slowly ascending in the process. The floor of the tunnel lacks much of the gravel and sand that was present in the cave below, and it is worn smooth in some places.

The tunnel leads up a total of 90 feet while ascending 40 feet in the process. A character that succeeds on a DC 12 Perception check while inspecting the floor will notice two small stone rat statues at the entrance to the cave. They are perfect simulations of the small rodents and are in fact victims of the cockatrice that lives in this cave.

The tunnel opens into a large cave with numerous stalactites and stalagmites that have grown together to form columns.

The cave itself is 100 feet long and more than 60 feet wide, with a tunnel exit leading to area D. The floor and ceiling have grown together with numerous stalactites and stalagmites forming columns around the room, forming a maze-like structure. Each round after the party enters the room, there is a 25% chance of encountering a large, purple and red chicken with hellish green eyes (a **cockatrice**).

The cockatrice has no real tactics, other than pecking at intruders until they stop moving and then feeding on the soft stone created by its horrible ability. There is no treasure here. The beast fears area D and will avoid it (having once been burned by an old trap).

Cockatrice CR 3
XP 800
HP 27 (Pathfinder Roleplaying Game Bestiary, "Cockatrice")

D. Tricks and Traps

The long, narrow cavern appears to have been carved from the stone rather than naturally formed like the previous caves. The ceiling is covered with stalactites, but the floors and walls are of smooth, carved stone. There is a thin layer of dust and stone fragments scattered across the floor.

Under the thin layer of detritus, you can just make out the diamond patterns on the square pavers that serve as the floor of this cave.

The cavern is 90 feet long and 30 feet wide. The floor is made of tightly-laid stone that has a diamond pattern etched on each of the 3-foot square stone pavers. Forty feet from the entrance from area C, there is evidence of scorching and soot staining covering a 10-foot-wide swath.

Note. Each of the following traps has a percentage chance to not function given their age and lack of upkeep. To determine if a trap will work, roll a d6. A roll of 1-2 on the d6 indicates that the particular trap in question does not activate.

Flame Jet Trap. An observant character that succeeds on a DC 10 Perception check while carefully examining the walls and floor near the soot-stained area of the cavern will discover nozzles deftly hidden at knee-height in the walls. They will also notice that the diamond patterns on the floor in this area are cleverly disguised pressure plates. The trap can be disabled by wedging an iron spike or other object under each of the pressure plates to prevent the trap from activating.

This flame jet trap is activated when a creature steps on one of the hidden pressure plates and a gout of flame erupts from the nozzles, scorching anyone in the 10-foot wide by 30-foot long area for 6d6 fire damage unless they succeed on a DC 13 Reflex saving throw.

Hidden Pit Trap. Twenty feet past the flame jet trap, at the 60-foot mark in the cavern, is a series of covered pits. Because each pit has a counterweight, each will only trigger if 100 pounds of weight is placed on the cover to each. If one of these traps is triggered, the floor (pit cover) swings open like a trapdoor, causing the creature to fall 20 feet to the bottom of the pit. The pit cover then quickly swings closed, trapping the creature in the dark, claustrophobic pit. A creature that falls into the pit takes 2d6 bludgeoning damage from the fall.

A successful DC 14 Perception check discerns that there is something slightly different about this section of the floor. A successful DC 14 Perception check is necessary to confirm that the section of the floor is actually the cover to several pits. Once detected, an iron spike can be wedged between the pit's cover and the surrounding floor in such a way as to prevent the cover from opening, thereby making it safe to cross. The cover can also be magically held shut using the *arcane lock* spell or similar magic.

Scythe Blade Trap. At the cavern exit, surrounding the diamond shape pattern on each floor tile that is directly in front of, and just inside, the exit (stepping on the diamond is safe, stepping outside the diamond on any of these floor tiles is not safe), are pressure plates that activate when 30 pounds of weight is placed on them, triggering a scything blade trap that cuts across the 10-foot exit tunnel. Any creature in this area must succeed on a DC 15 Reflex saving throw, taking 6d6 slashing damage on a failure.

Careful examination of the walls while succeeding on a DC 15 Perception check reveals the blades set between the stones of the walls on either side of the tunnel. The DC to spot the pressure plates is 15. With a successful DC 15 Perception check, a character can deduce the presence of the pressure plates from subtle variations in the mortar and stone used to create the plates compared to the surrounding pavers. Wedging and iron spike or other object under the pressure plates prevents them from activating. Spiking the troughs that house the blades will also prevent the trap from activating.

Overcoming the traps in this room rewards experience as a **CR 8** encounter (4,800 XP).

E. The Tomb

This small room has been completely finished with stonework. The walls are painted with intricate scenes and hieroglyphs of some ancient make. In the center of the chamber is a large sarcophagus made of stone. The top of the sarcophagus is intricately carved in the likeness of a human male of middle years.

The room itself is 30 feet square, with a 12-foot ceiling. A *comprehend languages* spell can discern that this is the tomb of a high priest of the god Set. The writing on the wall contains various unsavory scenes related to Set's dismembering of Osiris and of foul rites performed in his service. The writing contains a series of prayers to the dark god and promises from the deceased to serve Set in the underworld as he did in life.

The sarcophagus is 12 feet long and 5 feet wide. The lid is solid stone and is very heavy, requiring a DC 20 Strength check using crowbars or some other form of leverage to open. Inside are the mummified remains of the high priest of Set. On its face, the mummy wears a death mask of pure silver (1500 gp). Clasped in the mummy's hands, which are folded across its chest, is a golden broach inset with various semiprecious stones (250 gp). Near the mummy's feet are 6 canopic jars that are carved of various materials and intricately decorated (worth 100 gp each). Also near the mummy's feet is a large, thick tome. The tome is a *Tome of Understanding +1.* If the characters dump oil into the sarcophagus and set it ablaze immediately (thinking mummy, dried bandages, burn), the book is lost.

Although the mummy is inert, there is a curse on anyone disturbing the mummy's rest. One minute after any portion of the mummy or the canopic jars are removed from the sarcophagus, a Type I demon, a **vrock**, is summoned to the chamber. The demon fights for 1 minute then disappears.

Vrock CR 9
XP 6,400
HP 112 (Pathfinder Roleplaying Game Bestiary, "Demon, Vrock")

F. The Waterfall Chamber

This large cave is very wet and consists of many different pools and ledges that drop to lower pools. An underground river swiftly flows through the far side of the cavern.

The cavern itself is more than 300 feet in diameter with water flowing in from above (from area B as well as wilderness area 26). The underground river is at least 30 feet deep at its shallowest, with a very strong current that would easily sweep a creature away. No monsters or other dangers (other than possibly drowning or falling) are present.

You can either end the adventure here or add your own material to the cave. Perhaps there are multiple exits from the cave? Maybe the river leads deeper into the earth to areas that can be explored? Either way, this ends the module. We hope you have enjoyed it!

Appendix: Creatures and NPCs

Beaver, Giant — CR 1

XP 400
Giant beaver
N Medium animal
Init +0; **Senses** low-light vision; +6 Perception
AC 12, touch 10, flat-footed 12 (+2 natural)
hp 13 (2d8+5)
Fort +4, **Ref** +3, **Will** +0
Speed 20 ft., swim 30 ft.
Melee bite +3 (1d6+3)
Str 14, **Dex** 11, **Con** 13, **Int** 1, **Wis** 11, **Cha** 4
Base Atk +1; **CMB** +3; **CMD** 13 (17 vs. trip)
Feats Toughness
Skills Acrobatics +0 (-4 to jump), 6 Perception, Survival +1, Swim +10
SQ hold breath

Goblin Leader — CR 3

XP 800
Goblin unchained rogue 4
NE Small humanoid (goblinoid)
Init +2; **Senses** darkvision 60 ft.; Perception +7
AC 16, touch 13, flat-footed 14 (+3 armor, +2 Dex, +1 size)
hp 20 (4d8+4)
Fort +1, **Ref** +6, **Will** +1
Defensive Abilities danger sense +1, evasion, uncanny dodge
Speed 30 ft.
Melee dagger +4 (1d3+2/19-20), dagger +4 (1d3+1/19-20) or dagger +6 (1d3+2/19-20)
Ranged light crossbow +6 (1d6/19-20)
Special Attacks sneak attack (unchained) +2d6
Str 8, **Dex** 15, **Con** 10, **Int** 10, **Wis** 10, **Cha** 8
Base Atk +3; **CMB** +1; **CMD** 13
Feats Rapid Reload, Two-weapon Fighting, Weapon Finesse
Skills Acrobatics +8, Bluff +3, Climb +2, Disable Device +8, Escape Artist +8, Intimidate +3, Perception +7, Ride +5, Sense Motive +7, Sleight of Hand +8, Stealth +16, Swim +2; Racial Modifiers +4 Ride, +4 Stealth
Languages Goblin
SQ debilitating injury: bewildered, debilitating injury: disoriented, debilitating injury: hampered, rogue talents (fast getaway, fast stealth), trapfinding +2
Other Gear dagger, dagger, light crossbow, studded leather
Special Abilities
Debilitating Injury: Bewildered -2/-4 (Ex) Foe who takes sneak attack damage takes AC pen (more vs. striker) for 1 rd.
Debilitating Injury: Disoriented -2/-4 (Ex) Foe who takes sneak attack damage takes attack pen (more vs. striker) for 1 rd.
Debilitating Injury: Hampered (Ex) Foe who takes sneak attack damage has speed halved (and can't 5 ft step) for 1 rd.

Jasper the Leprechaun — CR 3

XP 800
Leprechaun unchained rogue 1
CN Small fey
Init +7; **Senses** low-light vision; Perception +18
AC 14, touch 14, flat-footed 11 (+3 Dex, +1 size)
hp 24 (5 HD; 4d6+1d8+6)
Fort +2, **Ref** +9, **Will** +6
DR 5/cold iron; **SR** 13
Speed 40 ft.
Melee dagger +7 (1d3+3/19-20)
Special Attacks sneak attack (unchained) +1d6
Spell-Like Abilities (CL 4th; concentration +7)
    Constant—shillelagh (DC 14)
    At will—dancing lights, ghost sound (DC 13), invisibility (self only), mage hand, major image (visual/auditory elements only) (DC 16), prestidigitation, ventriloquism (DC 14)
    3/day—color spray (DC 14), fabricate (1 cubic foot of material only)
    1/day—major creation
Str 7, **Dex** 16, **Con** 13, **Int** 14, **Wis** 15, **Cha** 16
Base Atk +2; **CMB** -1; **CMD** 12
Feats Improved Initiative, Slashing Grace, Weapon Finesse, Weapon Focus (dagger)
Skills Acrobatics +3 (+7 to jump), Appraise +6, Bluff +11, Escape Artist +11, Knowledge (nature) +10, Perception +18, Perform (comedy) +9, Perform (dance) +9, Sense Motive +10, Sleight of Hand +15, Stealth +15; Racial Modifiers +8 Perception, +4 Sleight of Hand
Languages Common, Elven, Halfling, Sylvan
SQ leprechaun magic, trapfinding +1
Other Gear dagger
Special Abilities
Leprechaun Magic (Sp) When a leprechaun uses any of its spell-like abilities to deceive, trick, or humiliate a creature (at the GM's discretion), the spell-like ability resolves at caster level 8th rather than 4th. If a leprechaun uses its spell-like abilities in this man

www.ingramcontent.com/pod-product-compliance
Lightning Source LLC
Chambersburg PA
CBHW041203100726
47911CB00016B/848